AGENT Amelia Ghost Diamond!

AGENT Amelia

Ghost Diamond!

Agent Amelia #1

MICHAEL BROAD

MINNEAPOLIS

American edition published in 2011 by Darby Creek, a division of Lerner Publishing Group, Inc.

First published in 2007 by Andersen Press Limited,
20 Vauxhall Bridge Road, London SW1V 2SA
www.andersenpress.co.uk
www.michaelbroad.co.uk

Darby Creek
A division of Lerner Publishing Group, Inc.
241 First Avenue North
Minneapolis, MN 55401 U.S.A.

Website address: www.lernerbooks.com

Library of Congress Cataloging-in-Publication Data

Broad, Michael.
    Ghost Diamond! / written and illustrated by Michael Broad. — American ed.
        v.   cm. — (Agent Amelia, #1)
    Summary: Elementary school secret agent Amelia continues her efforts to save the world from evil geniuses and criminal masterminds, this time foiling a jewel thief, identifying some unusual cat burglars, and evading a weed army.
    Contents: The case of the ghost diamond — The case of the cat-nappers — The case of the whispering weeds.
    ISBN: 978–0–7613–8056–6 (lib. bdg. : alk. paper)
    [1. Spies—Fiction. 2. Precious stones—Fiction. 3. Stealing—Fiction. 4. Cats—Fiction. 5. Burglary—Fiction. 6. Weeds—Fiction. 7. Scientists—Fiction] I. Title.
    PZ7.B780834Gho 2011
    [E]—dc22   2011002269

Manufactured in the United States of America
1 – BP – 7/15/11

For Shannon

I'M AMELIA KIDD and I'm a secret agent.

Well, I'm not actually a secret agent. I don't work for the government or anything. But I've saved the world loads of times from evil geniuses and criminal masterminds. There are loads of them around if you know what to look for.

I'm really good at disguises. I make my own gadgets (which sometimes work), and I'm used to improvising in sticky situations—which you have to do all the time when you're a secret agent.

These are my Secret Agent Case Files.

The Case of the Ghost Diamond

"What on earth do you have in that backpack?" Mom said. She leaned out of the car window as I heaved the bag off the backseat and onto my shoulders. It was pretty heavy, but I tried to pretend it wasn't.

"Stuff," I said. I peered over my sunglasses to gauge her reaction.

"Stuff!" Mom said, with a suspicious frown. And the way she said "stuff" meant she wanted to know exactly what kind of "stuff" and why I had so much of it.

"Just boring school-trip stuff." I smiled and headed for the school door.

Being vague is the best thing to do when you're under interrogation. Mom would have to really want to know what was in my bag to come after me and ask more questions, but

 I'd deliberately dawdled back at the house. I knew she was already running late.

You have to think ahead when you're a secret agent.

"Well, have a nice time then," Mom called out. Then she drove away.

Phew!

I couldn't tell Mom my bag was full of secret agent stuff. She'd think I'd gone bonkers. When you're a secret agent, you can't tell anyone.

They'd worry when you're off saving the world all the time. Especially my mom, who gets worried whenever I go anywhere on my own!

My class was
already boarding
the bus to take us
to the museum.

I stayed at the back and watched
our teacher, Ms. Granger, ticking
everyone off her list.

Ms. Granger had been under
my surveillance for a week. I was
pretty sure she was a criminal
mastermind posing as a teacher. I was
also pretty sure something weird was
about to go down at the museum.

Ms. Granger had planned the museum trip so our class could see the famous Ghost Diamond. It was a pendant containing the biggest diamond in the world. Usually school trips are educational, but the Ghost Diamond had nothing to do with our schoolwork. It didn't make sense. Then I snooped around the school library records and discovered Ms. Granger had recently

checked out two very suspicious-
sounding books.

One was called *Hypnotism for
Beginners,* and the other was called
Ancient Jewels and Curses.

The second one was a very
strange subject for a book. It was a bit
too much of a coincidence, if you ask
me!

My teacher was definitely up to something. I had to get to the bottom of it.

When it was my turn to board the bus, Ms. Granger blocked my way with her clipboard.

"Amelia Kidd, will you please take off those ridiculous sunglasses!" she shrieked. She shrieked it loud enough for the whole bus to hear, so everyone started giggling.

If Ms. Granger suspected me of being a secret agent, then she'd just done a very good job of drawing attention away from herself and to me. This is definitely the sort of thing an evil genius might do. I took off my sunglasses. Then Ms. Granger prodded my backpack with her clipboard.

"And what do you have in the bag?" she said. "The kitchen sink?"

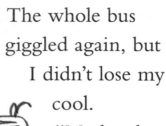

The whole bus giggled again, but I didn't lose my cool.

"My lunch and my big winter coat," I lied.

Well, I did have my lunch but not my winter coat. "Mom said I have to take a coat because it might turn chilly."

If a teacher starts questioning you, I've found it's a very good idea to blame everything on your mom. They can't say anything about it, and they never bother to phone and check.

"Sunglasses *and* a winter coat?" Ms. Granger said. She waved me onto the bus with an exhausted sigh. "Amelia Kidd, you really have come prepared!"

The other kids giggled again as I made my way down the aisle to the back of the bus. Under my breath, I said, "Yes, Ms. Granger, I've come prepared." I slipped my sunglasses back on.

Inside the museum I was keeping a close eye on Ms. Granger when I noticed she'd switched her shoes! She was wearing bright pink running shoes that looked very new. This was odd because the rest of her clothes were all dark and old-fashioned.

I'd never seen Ms. Granger wearing running shoes before.

She always wore
boring black shoes.
This was another
clue pointing to
something big
going down at
the museum.
I had to keep
alert and not
let my teacher
know I was on

to her. If she suspected me, she may
postpone her criminal activity for
another day.

"I like your shoes, Ms. Granger," said Trudy Hart. She's always kissing up to the teachers. I don't like Trudy Hart. She's very popular in school and is always mean to people who aren't, like me.

"Why, thank you, Trudy," said Ms. Granger. "They're new."

"They look very pretty on you," Trudy added with a slimy smile.

"Do you think so?" Ms. Granger smiled, turning her heel to admire the new running shoes. "Of course, field trips involve an awful lot of walking, so I'm wearing them mostly for comfort."

"Or to make a quick getaway!" I whispered.

Ms. Granger's head snapped up. She narrowed her eyes at me.

Uh-oh!

Ms. Granger told us to explore

the museum on our own. She gave
instructions to meet back at the gift
shop in an hour. After my comment
about the shoes, I knew she'd be
keeping an eye on me.
But I needed
to keep an eye
on her too.

I went straight to the ladies' room
and propped a trash can against the
door so I wouldn't be disturbed.

Then, in front of the mirror, I looked inside my backpack. I found a large flowery dress and a purple wig.

I pulled the dress on over my other clothes and tucked my hair inside the wig. I adjusted everything in the mirror. Once I didn't look like me anymore, I slipped my sunglasses back on and headed for the door.

BANG! BANG! BANG!

Someone was on the other side of the door trying to get in!

"Amelia Kidd!" said a loud, angry voice. "I demand you let me in this instant!"

It was Trudy Hart! And by the sound of giggling, I guessed she had a couple of her equally mean sidekicks with her. She must have seen me come in. With a quick glance at the barred windows, I realized I was completely trapped!

"My needs are greater than yours because I'm popular!" Trudy squealed and kicked the door.

I checked my disguise in the mirror again and wondered whether it would stand up to close scrutiny. Sometimes being a secret agent is all about thinking on your feet and taking chances. I pulled my shoulders back, grabbed my bag, and flung the door open.

"Well it's about time. . . ." Trudy growled. Then she stopped when she saw me.

"What a rude little girl!" I shrieked in my best grown-up voice. I eyed Trudy up and down. I prodded her with an authoritative finger. "I have a very good mind to find your teacher!"

29

Trudy's mouth fell open. Her sidekicks gawked at me with wide eyes.

Before any of
them could get a closer
look, I stormed past
like an angry adult.
They didn't say
anything or
come after
me. They were
definitely
fooled. Which
was good because
I really did have
to find the
teacher and figure out what she was
up to.

Did Ms. Granger plan to steal
the Ghost Diamond? And if so,
why? Criminal masterminds and evil
geniuses are only ever interested in

world domination. What could she want with a silly old pendant?

When I found Ms. Granger, she was leaving the gift shop with a small brown bag. This was very suspicious because she'd told everyone to meet there in an hour. Also, nobody goes to the gift shop first. Everyone goes afterward to buy souvenirs. You can't

buy a
souvenir of
somewhere
you haven't
properly
visited yet.

I hid
behind a
pillar until
Ms. Granger
passed me.
Then I followed
at a safe distance, ducking
and diving and blending into the
crowd. As I suspected, she was
heading for the room with the Ghost
Diamond. She was also looking
around her to make sure no one was
following.

Luckily, I'm used to tracking suspects so she didn't spot me.

In the Ghost Diamond room, I made two holes in a guidebook. Then I lurked close behind Ms. Granger. I watched her carefully as she studied the jewel. After a couple of minutes, she struck up a conversation with the security guard who was protecting the pendant.

". . . and why is it called the Ghost Diamond?" asked Ms. Granger casually.

Something told me she already knew and was just killing time. Or she was trying to distract the security

guard. But he was standing right next
to the jewel case. She couldn't do
anything without him
seeing.

The security
guard explained
that the white
center of the stone
was believed to
be the ghost of
a very powerful
spirit. The spirit
had vowed to rule
the world with any
person who released it
from the diamond prison.

Ding! Ding! Ding!
(That's the sound of alarm bells
ringing in my head.)

My instinct was right. Ms. Granger did want to rule the world. Now she was inches away from a strange diamond that would let her do exactly that!

While I was figuring all this out, I noticed that Ms. Granger had opened the brown bag from the gift shop. She was fiddling with something in her hands. But from where I stood, I couldn't actually see what she was doing.

Not wanting to risk getting closer, I rummaged inside my backpack. I pulled out my mirror-on-a-stick gadget. It sounds like an odd piece of secret agent equipment, but it has gotten me out of a lot of trouble in the past.

doing!

I positioned the mirror so I could get a close look at Ms. Granger's hands. I saw that she had an exact copy of the Ghost Diamond pendant! Ms. Granger must have picked it up in the gift shop. Now she was swinging it from side to side in a very peculiar way.

I was so busy watching my teacher I hadn't noticed the security guard. By this time, he had stopped talking and was staring at the fake pendant. He had a very glazed look in his eyes.

Hypnotism for Beginners! I gasped.

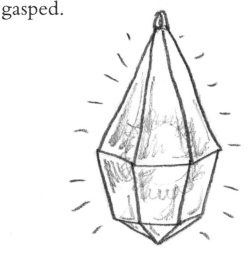

Ms. Granger turned around and gave me an angry glare. Then she sprang into action.

With the security guard too
hypnotized to notice, she smashed the
lid of the jewel case with her elbow.
Then she swapped the pendants and
escaped in her new
pink running shoes.

Shoving the
mirror back in
my backpack, I
chased after her.
The big dress
was weighing
me down a bit, and it
was kind of difficult
to see through the
long purple bangs of
my wig.

Ms.
Granger
was getting
away!

Up ahead I noticed Trudy Hart standing by the gift shop with her sidekicks. She was my only chance to stop Ms. Granger from getting away with the Ghost Diamond and taking over the world.

"Stop her!" I yelled at the top of my voice.

But Trudy just sneered and turned her nose up. I'm not sure whether she knew it was me or if she just didn't want to help the angry grown-up who had yelled at her earlier, but it was obvious she didn't intend to stop the sprinting teacher.

Ms. Granger was almost to the exit. I had to think fast.

Pulling the backpack off my shoulders, I swung it over my head to get up some speed. Then I threw it as hard as I could.

The bag sailed

through
.
the air . . .

. . . . and hit the floor at the teacher's
feet. The straps tangled around her
new pink running shoes.

Ms. Granger was running
one minute, and the next she
was sprawled on the floor. But
she continued to slide along
the shiny marble floor. She
was like a bowling ball
heading straight for Trudy
Hart and her sidekicks.
The girls watched in
horror. They were
frozen like pins in
a bowling alley
about to be
toppled.

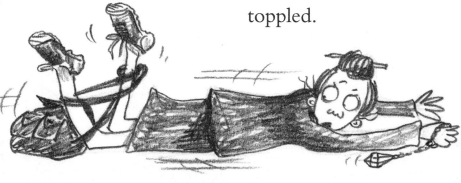

CRASH!

Skidding to a halt,
I snatched my backpack
from the heap of groaning
people and slipped away
just in time.

All the non-hypnotized security guards suddenly swooped on Ms. Granger. Because they weren't sure exactly what had happened, they pounced on Trudy Hart and her sidekicks too.

When you're a secret agent, you can't ever take credit for saving the world. If you did, everyone would know who you are and you wouldn't be secret anymore. So by the time I got back from the ladies' room, in my

normal clothes and with my normal
hair, Ms. Granger was being taken
away by the police.

All the kids in my class were
waiting on the steps of the museum.
I wandered cautiously over to Trudy
Hart and her sidekicks. They were all
looking a bit confused.

"What happened?" I said, with as much surprise on my face as I could fake.

One of Trudy's sidekicks burst into tears. Trudy rolled her eyes.

"Some crazy woman attacked Ms. Granger," she said, matter-of-factly.

"Oh," I said. "Then why are
they taking Ms. Granger away?"
Trudy scratched her head.

"I think maybe she stole
something from the gift shop?" she
said. It was obviously just a guess.
"I saw the security guards fighting
her for a necklace or something. She
seemed very angry."
"Oh," I said.

"The school has called our parents to come and collect us. . . ." Trudy added. Then she stopped and frowned at me. She lifted a hand up to my hair and pulled out a long purple hair!

Uh-oh!

I snatched it back and let the wind blow it away.

Trudy narrowed her eyes at me. She was about to say something when I heard the sound of a familiar car horn. I looked out to the road and saw Mom rolling down the window and waving.

"Gotta go!" I said. I dashed off before she could draw any conclusions.

I shoved my backpack onto the seat of the car and climbed in after it. Looking up at the museum steps, I could see Trudy Hart was still frowning. It looked like she was still trying to figure out what happened.

"I'm sorry your trip was cut short," Mom said, eyeing me in the mirror as we drove away. "Did you have time to see anything interesting at all?"

"I guess not," I said, tipping my glasses and peering over the top.

"And you carried that big bag around for nothing," Mom added sadly.

I thought about it for a moment
and then smiled to myself.

"Oh, I wouldn't say that,"
I said, patting my faithful old
backpack.

The Case of the Catnappers

"Amelia!" Mom yelled. "What on earth do you think you're doing?"

"Bird watching," I lied, without taking my eyes off the target.

"The point of binoculars is so you can see birds from the ground." Mom sighed. "You really don't need to be halfway up a tree. Now come down this instant before you snag your sweater!"

"OK,"
I said. "Just
one more
minute. I'm
watching
a very
interesting
bird."
I wasn't really
watching a
bird—I was
watching the
trap I'd set earlier.

Cats had been mysteriously
vanishing on my street. It began with
one, which wasn't too suspicious.
Cats wander off all the time. But
then another one disappeared,
followed by another. And within a

week, there were no cats left at all!

I was pretty sure a criminal mastermind was planning to take over the world using stolen cats. They're always doing tricky stuff like that. So I put my stuffed cat Tiddles out on the sidewalk as bait and waited for the catnapper to nab it.

Mom continued to moan in the background when a white van suddenly turned the corner into our street.

I watched as it slowed down outside our house. Then, quick as a flash, the back doors flew open.

An arm snatched Tiddles and the van screeched away!

I focused my binoculars on the speeding vehicle and saw the words "Smith's Fish" in blue lettering along the side.

The van belonged to the fish

shop around
the corner!
"Aha!" I
said. At last
I finally
had a
lead.
"Aha?"
Mom
asked, as I
clambered
down the branches.

"Oh, I was . . . watching an Aha
Bird building a nest," I said. "They're
very rare."

Mom frowned at my sweater and brushed pieces of bark and twigs away with her hand.

"I can't imagine why Gran agreed to knit you a black one," Mom sighed. "It really is the worst color for showing dust and things. And besides, black isn't very cheery for a girl of your age."

"I like it," I shrugged.

Of course my real reason for choosing black was that it would come in handy during nighttime stakeouts. Also, when you're up a tree in the daytime, a bright pink sweater would be a dead giveaway. You have to think ahead when you're a secret agent.

Mom was heading back to the house when I suddenly had an idea.

"Can we have fish for dinner tonight?" I asked, tagging along behind.

"But you don't like fish," she said. "The last time we had fish, you were ill."

"That was when I was little," I said. "I'm pretty sure I like it now."

"Hmmm, well, if you're sure," Mom said uncertainly. "But you'll have to go to the fish shop for me. I'm not going out again just because you've decided you like fish all of a sudden."

"OK," I said casually. I slipped on my sunglasses.

On the way to Smith's Fish, I
collected "LOST CAT" posters from
all the trees and lampposts. Now that
I knew who'd swiped the missing
kitties, I'd need a list of telephone
numbers to return them.

Outside the fish shop I tucked
the posters into my backpack and
rummaged around for an appropriate
disguise. Mom's mention of Gran had

already given me
an idea.

    I pulled on
an old raincoat,
crammed a short
curly wig on my
head, and tied a
see-through plastic
rain hood on top
of it. It wasn't

raining—but old ladies often wear rain hoods when it's not raining.

A bell rang as I tottered into Smith's Fish.

A short, plump man hurried out from the back of the shop and glared at me. I guessed this was Mr. Smith. He stood over the counter, folded his arms, and sighed.

Maybe he thought he had better things to do than serve old ladies— things like pinching people's pets!

"What do you want?" he demanded.

"I'd like some fish, please," I croaked, hunched over and gazing at the counter.

There wasn't a lot of fish to choose from, just a couple of shrimp and a crab. I guessed all the fish had been used up keeping the stolen cats happy. It must not be working, judging by the scratches on Mr. Smith's hands.

"What kind of fish do you want?" he asked impatiently.

"Two nice pieces of haddock, please," I said, peering over my sunglasses.

"We're all out of haddock," he snapped. "It's either shrimp, crab, or nothing."

"Oh, well in that case, I'll just have two nice pieces of haddock, please," I croaked. While Mr. Smith was busy getting angry, I surveyed the shop for any signs of cats. The great thing about the old-lady disguise is you can keep people distracted

for ages while you carry out basic surveillance.

"ARE YOU DEAF?" he yelled. "I SAID WE'RE ALL OUT OF HADDOCK!"

"Yes, haddock," I said. "Two nice pieces, please."

This went on for a while. Mr. Smith was getting very red in the face, when a short, plump woman appeared behind him. I figured this must be Mrs. Smith. She didn't look very happy either.

"What's going on out here?"
she growled, glaring sideways at her
husband.

"This deaf old lady wants
HADDOCK!" he growled back.

Mrs. Smith
offered me an
unconvincing
smile.

"Then fetch
some from the back!" she snarled.

"But . . ." said Mr. Smith.

"The job's going down tonight,
so we won't need it anymore," hissed
Mrs. Smith, through gritted teeth.

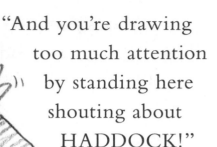

"And you're drawing too much attention by standing here shouting about HADDOCK!" The other great thing about the old-lady disguise is that people always think you're deaf. They think you can't hear them and always give away vital details.

Mrs. Smith gave me another fake smile, grabbed her husband by the elbow, and marched him out to the back of the shop. They started arguing. I couldn't hear everything,

but I did hear: "Keep a low profile!" and, "Get rid of her!"

The reason I couldn't hear them properly was because I'd leaped over the counter.

I was busy rummaging through a pile of papers. I was looking for clues to the exact location of the cats.

Among the bills and receipts, I found a strange map!

I didn't have time to look properly, but I did see the word *cat* among the various scribbles. Deciding the map must lead to the cats, I shoved it in my raincoat and crept back around the counter.

Mr. Smith suddenly reappeared with a parcel wrapped in white paper.

"Two nice pieces of haddock, ma'am," he said politely.

I didn't get a chance to study the map before dinner, so that evening I pretended to have an upset tummy. I asked to go to bed early.

"I knew I shouldn't have let you have fish," Mom sighed.

I shrugged my shoulders helplessly and shuffled off to my room.

Closing my bedroom door carefully, I ran to the desk, flicked on the lamp, and unfolded the piece of paper. On closer inspection, I discovered it wasn't a map at all. It was a blueprint.

A blueprint of the local bank!

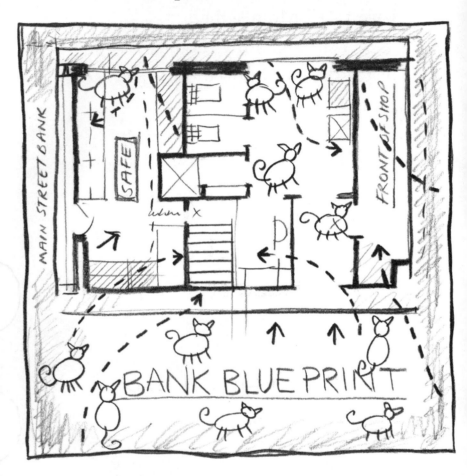

There was a diagram over the
blueprint with drawings of cats and

arrows pointing in and out of the bank. I couldn't figure out exactly how, but it was clear the Smiths had stolen the cats so they could rob a bank!

It surprised me that Mr. and Mrs. Smith were only robbing a bank and not planning to take over the world. Everything about them said criminal mastermind to me. Then I turned the paper over and found a note scribbled in the corner.

"After robbery— steal more cats and then TAKE OVER THE WORLD!"

I knew it!

I also knew from Mrs. Smith's careless

whispering that the job was going down tonight. I didn't have much time. I stuffed my backpack full of gadgets. I dressed in black pants, black sweater, and a black cap. Then

I shimmied down the downspout and headed straight for Main Street.

I got to the bank just as Mr. and Mrs. Smith pulled up in their van.

Diving into
a nearby
doorway,
I watched
from the
shadows
as Mrs.
Smith tiptoed around the back of
the vehicle. She flung the rear doors
open and clapped her
hands twice.
Suddenly
dozens of
cats spilled
from the
van and
gathered
around
her feet.

Mrs. Smith pulled a piece of fish from her pocket and whistled through her fingers. All the cats immediately sat bolt upright and gazed at her intently. Then she

whistled again, and they formed an orderly line outside the bank.

The cats had all been trained!

I watched in amazement as the woman crouched down and began whistling a series of complicated commands. Each pair of furry ears

twitched in turn as she gave the
cats their instructions and a small
piece of fish. Then she stood up
and pointed to the bank.
Suddenly all the cats
sprang into action. Some
scaled the downspout. Others
climbed up to the first-floor
windows. And a couple of the
smaller ones clambered through
the bank's deposit
box. Each cat found its
own way inside the bank
until there
were none
left on the
sidewalk
beside Mrs.
Smith.

Mr. Smith
stayed in the
van the whole
time revving the
engine. He was
obviously the getaway
driver. But that also meant
that once the cats returned, the
Smiths would speed away with all the
cats and the loot!

I decided there was no way
to stop the van without getting
squashed. I had to somehow prevent
the animals from returning to
the van. And I had to think fast
because the first of the cat burglars
had already returned—followed by
another, then another . . . .

Some of the cats had wads of

money in their
mouths. Others
were holding
bags of coins.
A few were
even wearing
diamond tiaras

and matching
necklaces. They
looked very pleased with themselves!

Mrs. Smith stood among them and seemed to be counting heads.

I rummaged frantically in my backpack for a gadget that might help me out. I needed something to create a diversion or lure the cats away. But there was nothing appropriate.

Then I glanced down at my sweater. . . .

Quick as a flash, I snagged a thread. I pulled a long length of yarn from my sleeve and leaped from my hiding place.

"Here, puss-puss!" I shrieked.

Waving my arm in the air, I dashed past a startled Mrs. Smith and through the pack of cats. I twitched and dangled the yarn over their bobbing heads.

As I'd hoped, they started
leaping up and swiping at the yarn
with their paws.

I definitely had their attention.
Before Mrs. Smith could figure out
what was happening, I escaped down
the street trailing the yarn behind
me. The cats followed me, leaving
Mrs. Smith alone outside the bank
with her mouth hanging open.

Mr. Smith honked the horn,
and his wife jumped back into the
van. With a sudden shrieking of tires,
they chased me—and the trail of rich
kitties—down the street.

Mr. Smith was waving his
fist in the air, and Mrs. Smith was
hanging out of the window clapping
and whistling frantically. Luckily, the
cats were more interested in the yarn

and completely ignored them. But
the van was quickly gaining.

I turned into the nearest alley
and heard the van screech to a halt
behind me. Mr. and Mrs. Smith
leaped out. They started chasing on
foot. Glancing back, I saw their faces

were very red. I wasn't sure if it was anger or because they were both short and plump and not used to running.

I had to think fast!

With no time to open my backpack, I looked down at my sweater again.

The yarn from my right sleeve was still trailing behind me, so I started unraveling the left one. I pulled out great long loops of yarn one after the other. By the time I reached the street, I had a big armful of tangled yarn.

I turned the corner and
crouched behind the wall.

The cats gathered around my
feet tapping the limp thread half–
heartedly, when suddenly the panting
couple staggered out of the alley. I
immediately jumped up and threw
the tangle of yarn over their heads
like a big, black spiderweb.

With the excitement of so much dangling yarn, the cats went nuts again and started jumping all over the place. They swiped at anything that moved. They mostly swiped at Mr. and Mrs. Smith, who were trying to snatch the cash.

"**Ow!**" said Mr. Smith.

"**Meow!**" said the cats.

"**Ow!**" said Mrs. Smith.

"**Meow!**" said the cats.

In
all the
confusion,
I circled the fishy
couple as fast as I
could. I
wound yarn around
their arms and
legs like a spider
wrapping a fly. The
more their greedy hands grabbed for
the loot, the more entangled they
became.

Eventually I ran out of
yarn and there was
nothing left of my
black sweater,
but by this
time,

the catnappers were just a big, black blob. They were so knotted up that they couldn't move an inch.

The cats were still swiping at loose yarn dangling from the wrapped-up crooks when I noticed people were stopping to see what was going on. It must have seemed very peculiar.

When you're a secret agent, you can't take credit for saving the world all the time. If you did, you wouldn't be secret anymore. So I pulled my hat down over my face while I worked out what to do next.

Police sirens wailed in the distance, but I couldn't stick around to explain what had happened.

I had to think fast.

Squinting through the wool of my hat, I rummaged inside my backpack again. I was desperately looking for a gadget that might get me out of another sticky situation.

Instead, I found the "LOST CAT" posters and the bank blueprint!

"Aha!" I said

I pulled some loose yarn from the tangle and attached the blueprint firmly to the heads of Mr. and Mrs. Smith. Then I stuck all the "LOST CAT" posters around the whole bundle. The police would definitely need to know who to phone once they'd rounded up the kidnapped cats.

Now that the case was completely solved, I pulled on my backpack and disappeared into the night (in true secret agent style). I did bump into a few people on the way because I couldn't really see where I was going.

I managed to sneak back into my room without Mom knowing.

The next day I got into a little
trouble for "losing" my black sweater.
Mom didn't make a big deal about
it, though. I think she was secretly
pleased.

In fact, Mom was so not
annoyed that she rushed out and
bought a bundle of bright pink yarn.
Then Gran set to work knitting me a
brand-new sweater.

Which was
OK, because
I like pink ...
when I'm not
busy being a
secret agent.

The Case of the Whispering Weeds

"Must you carry that big backpack everywhere you go, Amelia?" Mom asked. I climbed into the backseat of the car. "I really can't imagine what you think you need. We're only going to the garden center for plant food for my roses. What's in there?"

"Just dolls," I lied, peering over my sunglasses.

Mom rolled her eyes as we drove away. She started giving me a lecture about how I was too old to be

playing with dolls. She said I should make some real friends.

My backpack was actually full of secret agent equipment, but I couldn't tell Mom. She'd worry about me. Saving the world can be dangerous, and Mom was definitely better off thinking I was playing with dolls.

I was on a secret
mission to investigate
suspicious activity
going on at the
garden center.
Sightings
of strange
creatures—
stuff like
that. But
it was too far away for me to bike.
So every night after school, I crept
into the garden to sabotage Mom's
rosebushes. I'm not proud of it. I
didn't do any real damage. I just had
to make sure they looked sad and
droopy by the weekend.

You have to think ahead when
you're a secret agent.

I thought I was prepared for
anything when we reached the
garden center, but I hadn't expected
to run into Trudy Hart! Trudy is in
my class, and we don't get along.

"Isn't that your friend?" Mom
asked, when she spotted Trudy. She
was wandering through the leafy
aisles with her dad. Mom must have

seen Trudy and me arguing at school or something and guessed we were friends.

"No," I said flatly. "She's really not."

"Yoo-hoo!" Mom shrieked. She grabbed my arm and pulled me over to Trudy and her dad. They were arguing over plants. It sounded like Trudy wanted only pink flowers in the garden. She was giving her dad a really hard time about it.

Trudy and I glared at each other. Our parents decided she and I should go off together to look at flowers. We'd all meet at the checkout lane in an hour. Mom was clearly delighted that I'd be spending time with a real person instead of a doll. Trudy's dad seemed only too pleased to dump her on me.

Parents always think that just because another kid is the same age, you should have no problems being best friends with them. They don't even think about whether you have anything in common. Trudy and I have nothing in common. She's really popular at school. I don't have time to be popular because I'm too busy saving the world all the time.

"'Bye, then," I said to Trudy, as soon as we were out of sight of our parents.

"Yeah, good riddance!" snapped Trudy.

At the end of the aisle, Trudy went one way, and I went the other.

I had an investigation to carry out. I couldn't risk Mom and Trudy

seeing me in secret agent mode—or
interfering while I'm trying to save
the world. So I hid behind a large
potted fern and searched inside my
backpack.

I pulled on a big yellow
summer dress over my clothes.
I tucked my hair under a frizzy
blonde wig, and then I crammed

a big floppy sun hat
on top. I could hardly
see through the frizzy
bangs and the brim
of the hat. I hoped
that meant no
one would
recognize me.

Turning the
corner, my disguise
was immediately put to the test. I ran
straight into Mom!

"Why, I have that exact same
dress!" Mom said.
It's no
wonder she
recognized it.
It was Mom's
dress!

But I couldn't stand and talk about it. Mom might also recognize her floppy sun hat and realize it was me.

"This old rag?" I shrieked, in my best impression of an old woman's voice. "It's hideous. I only ever use it for gardening!" And with that, I grabbed the nearest plant. I barged past Mom like I was the rudest woman in the world.

"Well, really!" Mom exclaimed,
shaking her head angrily.

I quickly put the plant into
a nearby cart. I whizzed off to the
opposite end of the garden center.
There I set to work looking for
clues. I filled the cart as I went
along like a real shopper would do.

You have to blend in when you're carrying out surveillance. It looks odd if you're just sneaking around.

I also had to keep an eye out for Mom and Trudy!

After half an hour of searching,
I still hadn't found anything
suspicious in the garden center. With
only the greenhouse section left,
I was beginning to think nothing
weird was going on after all.

I made my way slowly through the aisles of greenhouses. I felt bad about making Mom's roses droopy for nothing. Then something suddenly shot across my path!

I froze on the spot, tipped my sunglasses, and scanned the floor. I hadn't seen exactly what it was because it moved too fast. But it was bigger than a mouse, and it moved like a small, dark octopus!

Crouching down, I noticed a faint line of dirt on the white-tiled floor! Whatever it was, the creature had left a trail!

I immediately turned my cart and set off after it. I was so busy watching the trail of dirt that I didn't notice when a man

leaped out in front of my cart! I dug my heels into the floor, but it was too late.

CRASH! OOPS!

"Look where you're going, you silly old fool!" the man growled. He picked himself up from the floor and patted the dust from his garden center uniform. He was tall and thin and very mean-looking.

The man obviously mistook me for an old lady.

I was hunched over and staring at the floor. So I went along with it and kept my face well hidden beneath the hat.

"Oh! Dearie me!" I croaked. "I'm terribly sorry, young man."

"And you should be!" He snapped. "There are some very rare plants in this department!" The man shook his fist angrily. Then he stormed away mumbling under his breath.

I decided it was very strange that the man had been so rude. People who work in shops are supposed to be nice to the customers, even if they mow you down with their carts. His comment about rare plants was even stranger. There didn't seem to be any plants at all in this department, just aisles of empty greenhouses.

Hmmm.

I kept an eye out for the strange man and found the trail of dirt again.

Before long the trail stopped outside one of the greenhouses. This greenhouse was right at the back of the showroom and was different from the rest. It was bigger and older, and it was also clouded over with condensation. Nothing could be seen through the hazy panes of glass.

Leaving the cart in the aisle, I pushed the glass

door open and peered inside. The greenhouse was hot and humid and full of plants. But they weren't rare

plants. All the plants in the misty greenhouse looked just like weeds!

I stepped inside and glanced around.

None of the plants were in pots or bedding trays. They were definitely weeds. And they were scattered all over the floor as if someone had just weeded out their garden and dumped them there.

What was going on?

Reaching inside my backpack, I pulled out my extendable grabber-hand gadget. (It's basically a hand on a stick.) Whatever had scuttled across my path must be hiding under the weeds. I didn't want to use my real hand just in case the mysterious creature had teeth!

After a few minutes of careful poking, I found nothing among the

weeds. I had to stop to catch my
breath. The greenhouse was as hot as
an oven, and I was baking under the
dress, hat, and wig.

Then I realized no one could
see me through the misted glass
of the greenhouse. I peeled off my
damp disguise and packed it away.

But when I crouched
down to refasten
my backpack, I
suddenly heard
a strange sound
coming from the
weeds.

At first, it
sounded like the
kind of hissing
that grass makes
when it's blown by
the breeze. After
listening carefully,
it began to sound
more and
more like
whispering.

It sounded like the weeds were talking to one another!

Then I realized something dreadful.

The creature I'd been tracking wasn't under the weeds. The creature *was* the weeds. And I was trapped in a greenhouse with a great big pile of them!

Uh-oh!

The weeds stopped whispering and slowly began to move. The roots and leaves gathered around my feet. Some of the more stringy ones tried to wrap their vines around my shoes!

I jumped back with a gasp.

The weeds immediately started whispering again. They spread out across the floor of the greenhouse like soldiers. Suddenly they leaped up on their roots like little white legs.

They scuttled after me waving their leaves angrily in the air.

"ARRRRRGGGGHHH!" I screamed. Screaming isn't the sort of thing you're supposed to do when you're a secret agent, but they were really creepy, and they took me by surprise.

I threw the door open and was about to escape when I saw a tall, thin figure blocking my path! It was the man I'd knocked over with my cart, and he was smiling at me.

But it wasn't a
friendly smile. It was
an I'm-going-to-rule-
the-world smile. I've
seen it loads of times
before. Criminal
masterminds and
evil geniuses
always have an
I'm-going-to-
rule-the-world smile.

"So you found my
rare plants?"
he chuckled.

I glanced
back at the
weeds. They
were still
standing

on their roots, but they'd stopped scuttling. They seemed to be looking up at the man as if waiting for instructions.

The best thing to do when confronted by criminal masterminds or evil geniuses is to keep cool and not let them know you're scared. It was difficult, especially knowing the whispering weeds were right behind me, but I gave the man my best fearless glare.

"You won't get away with this!"
I growled and waved my extendable
grabber-hand at him.

"Won't get away with what?"
asked the man, frowning at my
gadget.

"With . . . whatever it is you're
trying to get away with!" I said. I
still wasn't sure exactly what the man
was up to with his creepy weedy
army. But I was expecting a big,
long rant about taking over the
world. That's what criminal
masterminds and evil
geniuses always do.

"You're too late, little girl!" the thin man said. "My troops are ready! Once dispatched, they will creep into every garden and spread into every field and farm in the world. . . . "

If evil geniuses and criminal masterminds didn't spend so much time ranting about their plans to take over the world, they'd probably be a lot more successful. But they love bragging about how clever they are. So I used the time to look for a way to stop him.

My eyes fell on my shopping cart sitting in the aisle behind him.

". . . My weed army will control every crop on the planet!" he continued. "Then I will hold the whole world for ransom!"

With one careful flick of my grabber-hand, I extended it behind the man and into the cart. I flicked a big clay flowerpot up in the air and dropped it on his head.

"OW!" The man growled, rubbing the top of his head angrily.

It didn't knock him out, but he was distracted long enough for me to run past.

I grabbed the handle of the cart and ran as fast as I could.

The cart had filled up quite a bit while I was pretending to be a shopper. It quickly picked up speed. Once it was going fast enough, I leaped into the basket and rode it through the aisles of greenhouses.

Looking back, I saw the man stoop down to whisper to the weed army gathered at his feet. Then he nodded in my direction, and the weeds suddenly started chasing me!

They shot across the floor hissing and waving their leaves.

Rummaging inside the cart for stuff to throw at them, I found two green spray bottles.

I lifted them out and was about to
lob them at the weeds when I saw
the labels on the bottles.

EXTRA-STRENGTH
WEED KILLER!

Squirt!

Squirt!

        I quickly
flicked the caps off the
bottles, curled my fingers
around the triggers, and as the first
of the weeds leaped into the air, I
squirted them!

They instantly fell away,
landing with a splat, but the others
kept on coming.

Squirt! Squirt! Squirt!

As the last angry weed splatted
on the floor in a limp, mushy heap,

Squirt!

Squirt!

I looked back at the thin man. Needless to say, he'd lost his I'm-going-to-rule-the-world smile. It was now replaced with the equally familiar my-life's-work-is-ruined frown!

He wouldn't be causing any
trouble now!

I was about to feel pleased with
myself for saving the world again.
Then I suddenly realized I was still
sitting in a cart moving quickly
through the aisles of the garden
center.

Uh oh!

I leaped off the cart and grabbed the handle. Digging my heels into the floor, I managed to steer to avoid one crash. Unfortunately, I sent the cart hurtling around the corner and into the main section of the garden center!

Still
holding on,
I was dragged by
the cart through the leafy
aisles. Suddenly I heard a thud and a
very startled "yelp!"

I peered over the top of the handle and saw a very dazed Trudy sitting in the cart. Her arms and legs were hanging over the sides. Picking up an unexpected passenger definitely slowed the cart down, but peering through Trudy's legs, I saw something ahead. We were heading straight for it.

It was the checkout lane, and standing beside it were Mom and Trudy's dad.

They both looked up at the same time, and their mouths fell open.

CRASH! OOPS!

On the way home in the car, Mom was silent. She usually gives me the silent treatment when she's really angry. It happens quite a lot because saving the world often gets me into trouble.

In fact, Mom only spoke once during the whole trip home.

"That girl Trudy is clearly a very bad influence on you. I don't want to see you hanging around with her again," Mom growled. She shook her head at the memory of Trudy and me crashing into the cash register and smashing the cart.

"OK," I said. This was a bit of a bonus.

"And on second thought," Mom added, glancing back at my bulging backpack, "perhaps you *are* better off playing with your dolls. They're definitely a lot less dangerous!"

AGENTAmelia

Check out my other books!

#1 Ghost Diamond
#2 Zombie Cows
#3 Hypno Hounds
#4 Spooky Ballet

Three more fabulously funny stories in each book.